This Walker book belongs to:

First published 1993 by Walker Books Ltd
87 Vauxhall Walk, London SE11 5HJ

This edition published 2008

2 4 6 8 10 9 7 5 3 1

Printed in China

British Library Cataloguing in Publication Data:
a catalogue record for this book is available from the British Library.

ISBN 978-1-4063-1672-8

www.walkerbooks.co.uk

Hide and Seek

1 2 3
4 5 6 7
8 9 10

Jez Alborough

WALKER BOOKS
AND SUBSIDIARIES

LONDON · BOSTON · SYDNEY · AUCKLAND

I'm Frog.
I'm playing hide and seek
with my friends,

I'm playing hide and seek
with my friends,

but I can't see anyone.
Can you?

but Hippo and I
can't see anyone.
Can you?

I'm playing hide and seek
with my friends,

but Hippo, Snake and I
can't see anyone.
Can you?

I'm playing hide and seek
with my friends,

but Hippo, Snake, Tortoise and I can't see anyone. Can you?

I'm playing hide and seek
with my friends,

but Hippo, Snake, Tortoise, Toucan and I can't see anyone. Can you?

Now where's Frog?
We can't see him anywhere.
Can you?